TO: Lucas, Titi,
lili

Gracias por Ser
parte de esta
aventura !!

Con Amor, Señor David

David Rodriguez III

10/7/18

♡

The Many Adventures Of
BRUISER
The Jack Russell Terrier

By David Rodriguez III

Halo
PUBLISHING
INTERNATIONAL

ISBN: 978-1-61244-644-8
Library of Congress Control Number: 2018906466

Printed in the United States of America

Halo Publishing International
1100 NW Loop 410
Suite 700 - 176
San Antonio, Texas 78213
1-877-705-9647
www.halopublishing.com
contact@halopublishing.com

I dedicate this book to my parents and to my younger brother. Thank you for your tremendous love and support and for always believing in me. This book is also dedicated to my dog Bruiser, for inspiring me to write a story that's not too far from the truth. I love you!

4

Early one morning while Mr. David was getting ready for work, Bruiser dragged himself out of bed and did his first stretch of the morning. As he waited for his morning treat, he thought, *I need an adventure!*

Bruiser jumped onto the counter, grabbed Mr. David's car keys, and buried them in his dog bed.

"Hmmm, that's odd. Where did my keys go?" Mr. David wondered to himself.

"Found them!" Mr. David announced as he raced toward the door. He grabbed the backpack. "Woah, this bag is heavy! I should clean it out this evening."

During the drive to Mr. David's preschool, Bruiser thought about all the fun he was going to have and how careful he would have to be so that he would not get caught.

Bruiser peaked out from the backpack—and jumped! He raced for the hallway, and Mr. David didn't even have a chance to see him.

As he strolled down the hall, Bruiser was in complete amazement. He admired the brightly colored butterflies hanging from the ceiling. There were many different types of artwork, from mosaics to finger paintings that colored the walls.

6

In one classroom, a teacher announced, "Boys and girls, here are plain sheets of paper that we are going to use for finger painting!"

Bruiser's ears perked up, and he tiptoed into the classroom. One boy was painting alone, and Bruiser snuck in to join the fun.

The boy smiled at Bruiser. "Hi, I'm Ben! Are you going to paint with me?"

"Nice to meet you, Ben. I'm Bruiser," the dog replied. "I'm going to paint a giant green dinosaur and an enormous, purple spaceship with twinkling yellow stars."

"That sounds great, Bruiser!" Ben replied excitedly.

Bruiser grabbed different bottles of paint and splattered them all over the easel. He was working so hard on his masterpiece that paint ended up on the floor, the classroom walls, the fish tank, the windows, and all over Bruiser's fur.

Suddenly, a loud gasp sounded through the classroom. "Ben!" the teacher shouted.

Bruiser rocketed out of his seat and, in the blink of an eye, he was out of the classroom entirely.

"Look at this giant mess you have created with the paint!" Ben's teacher exclaimed. "You have lost your recess privileges. You will have to tidy up this mess later."

Bruiser raced down the hall, feeling bad for getting Ben in trouble. Before he could go back and apologize, he overheard a teacher mention a "science experiment." His ears perked up again, and Bruiser weaseled his way into another classroom.

Once inside he found a seat by a young girl. "Hi! I'm Bruiser!"

"Nice to meet you, Bruiser. I'm Sally," she replied.

While Sally's teacher explained the rules to the class, Bruiser made silly faces, distracting Sally from making the proper measurements for the volcano experiment.

When it came time to try the experiment, Bruiser added more water, a lot more vinegar, and much more baking soda to his volcano. Sally tried to stop Bruiser, but he could not resist. Bruiser and Sally stepped back as their volcano expanded. . . and expanded.

BOOM!

Foam burst out of the volcano and filled the entire room. Everyone was covered, and Bruiser made yet another grand escape just as the teacher said, "Sally if you were unsure of the correct measurements, you should have asked for help!"

"But it wasn't my fault! I was distracted by a wiry-haired dog named Bruiser."

"Sally, I don't see a dog in this classroom. What have I told you about fibs?" Her teacher shook her head. "During recess you'll have to help me wipe down all the foam from the classroom."

Bruiser snuck away, distracted from Sally and the foam by a calm and tidy classroom. Inside, the teacher and a few students were building a LEGO castle, which was going great, until Bruiser noticed a basket of brightly colored balls.

Bruiser strolled in, passing right by the teacher. He picked a ball from the basket and started tossing it in the air. A small group of students came over to watch him play. Then, Bruiser picked up two more balls and started juggling.

"WOW!" shouted a boy. "That's awesome!"

His teacher was preoccupied with the LEGO castle and didn't notice the kids watching Bruiser's tricks. As more kids came to watch, Bruiser began adding more balls and juggling them while standing on one paw.

The kids cheered and hollered. "More! More!" they cried. Bruiser jumped on top of the globe, juggling while racing over each continent.

But Bruiser was running out of breath. He lost his balance —catapulting over the teacher's head and straight into the LEGO castle!

CRASH!

Bruiser rustled through the bits of LEGO bricks, racing out of the classroom before the teacher could see him.

"Oh no!" the teacher cried, "What happened, Henry?"

Henry replied, "A small white dog with short little legs did it! He sure is fast and good at juggling."

"Henry, that's nonsense. During recess, you'll stay inside and help me reorganize the LEGOs."

"Yes, ma'am," Henry replied.

While Bruiser strolled down the halls looking for more fun, he noticed a line of kids going outside. He followed them into a garden that was full of blooming sunflowers, daisies, and ripe vegetables like tomatoes, squash, and peppers.

One girl smiled at him. "Hi! I'm Sydney. What are you doing here?"

"I'm looking for a bone," Bruiser replied. He dug through the soil, wiggling through all the neat rows and stepping on some of the plants.

"BRUISER!" Sydney cried. "You need to clean up the mess you made in our vegetable garden!"

"But I need to check the sandbox for bones," Bruiser replied.

Sydney hollered at Bruiser again. "I'm not going to take the blame for this torn up garden, but I can help you put it back the way you found it. How does that sound?"

"I guess that's good," Bruiser huffed.

Sydney and Bruiser replanted the garden. They put the sunflowers back in place and helped to perk up the daisies. Finally, they weeded and watered the garden.

As Sydney and Bruiser were walking side by side to the playscape, Bruiser noticed a few kids were sitting out during recess. "Sydney, why are some of the students sitting out while everyone else is playing?"

"Some of the students got blamed for the paint splatter all over the classroom, the volcano eruption, and for knocking over the class's LEGO castle, and they all blamed it on. . ." Sydney looked at Bruiser, her eyes widening. "Bruiser, were you responsible for all three classroom disasters?"

"I'm sorry. I should have told the teachers that I was the one who created the messes. I have to make it up to them!"

Bruiser raced towards the door. First, he grabbed a sponge and bucket and cleaned up the paint that was splattered in Ben's classroom, before tackling the foam in Sally's room.

Lastly, he went to Henry's classroom and assembled the LEGO castle, and he even added a few extra touches that he thought the kids would enjoy.

Before he made his grand escape, he posted a letter in the teacher's lounge.

DEAR TEACHERS,

I DO APOLOGIZE FOR:

1. NOT CLEANING UP THE PAINT I SPLATTERED
2. CREATING A FOAMY MESS FROM THE VOLCANO
3. KNOCKING OVER THE LEGO CASTLE

I AM THE ONE TO BLAME, NOT BEN, SALLY, OR HENRY. I SHOULD HAVE MADE BETTER DECISIONS. I HOPE THAT YOU WILL LET ME VISIT THE SCHOOL AGAIN. I SURE HAD LOTS OF FUN IN YOUR CLASSROOMS.

SINCERELY, BRUISER

(THE WIRY-HAIRED, SMALL WHITE DOG WITH LITTLE FEET)

Dear Teachers,

I do apologize for:

1. Not cleaning up the paint I splattered
2. Creating a foamy mess from the volcano
3. Knocking over the LEGO castle

I am the one to blame, not Ben, Sally or Henry. I should have made better decisions. I hope that you will let me visit the school again. I sure had lots of fun in your classrooms.

Sincerely,
Bruiser
(The wiry-haired, small white dog with little feet)

22

Bruiser felt pleased for telling the truth and making everything better. He walked out of the preschool and strolled back home for his afternoon nap.

When Mr. David came home from work, he sat beside his furry little friend on the couch. "There was a funny note in the teacher's lounge when I left. Sounds like someone was stirring up trouble at school. Do you know anything about that?" Mr. David asked with a smirk.

Bruiser stood up and stretched, before lying down on Mr. David's lap. "Good boy," Mr. David replied.

CPSIA information can be obtained
at www.ICGtesting.com
Printed in the USA
BVHW02*1800080718
521105BV00006B/8/P

9 781612 446448